Ella's Got Talent

GROSSET & DUNLAP
Penguin Young Readers Group
An Imprint of Penguin Random House LLC

Based on "Ella's Got Talent" from the animated television series *Ella the Elephant*. Story by Sheila Dinsmore. Teleplay by J. D. Smith.
ELLA THE ELEPHANT™ and all related logos and characters are trademarks of DHX Cookie Jar Inc.
Ella the Elephant © 2013 CJ Ella Productions Inc. DHX MEDIA® DHX Media Ltd.

dhx

ISBN 978-1-101-99499-3

10 9 8 7 6 5 4 3 2 1

Ella's teacher, Mrs. Briggs, told her class they were going to put on a talent show. Everyone was so excited! Frankie said he was going to show off his Boom-Boom-Kazoomba-Trombu-lele.

"It's the greatest one-man band ever invented!" he explained. "Now I just have to learn how to play it!"

Frankie's friends laughed.

3

Ada and Ida planned
on singing a duet.

Belinda was going to star
in a fancy dance routine!

Ella wasn't sure what to do for the talent show.

"What if you don't know what you're talented at?" she asked Mrs. Briggs after class.

"Oh, Ella, you shine in so many ways!" her teacher answered. "I'm sure you'll find your talent soon. In the meantime, could you write an introduction for each act? You're so good with words!"

On the way home from school, Tiki asked Ella what she was going to do for the talent show. Ella said she wasn't sure, but that she would decide soon. Tiki said she was going to put on a shadow-puppet show.

Since Ella didn't know what she was going to perform yet, Belinda asked her if she'd like to help her practice dancing.

Bump! Ella fell on the ground. Maybe ballet wasn't Ella's talent!

Belinda told Ella that she was working on a new dance routine. When Ella heard that, she came up with the perfect name: the Beautiful Belinda Blue and Her Banana Ballet!

"I love it!" Belinda said.

Then Ella visited Ada and Ida.

"Let's see if your hidden talent is singing," said Ada. "Let's try some scales."

"*La, la, la, la, la, la,*" Ella attempted to sing. "I don't think I'm cut out for singing," she admitted. "Especially with the famous Seeing Double in the show!"

The twins loved the name that Ella had invented for them.

Ella visited Frankie next.

   She tried to play the kazoo, but she didn't think music was her talent, either. She did have an idea for how to introduce Frankie, though: the one, the only, Frankie on his Boom-Boom-Kazoomba-Trombu-lele!

The next day, Ella gave Mrs. Briggs the introductions she'd written for the talent show.

"These are so clever, Ella!" said Mrs. Briggs. "Did you figure out what your talent is?"

"Not really. I think I'll just help out backstage," Ella answered.

That night, Ella and her friends
gathered backstage for the performance.
"Is everyone ready for our big show?"
Ella asked.

14

Tiki thought she was ready, but suddenly she noticed that something was missing.

"I can't find my music! I think I left it at home. I can't go on without my music!" she said worriedly.

When they saw the program, Ada and Ida started getting concerned, too.

"Is Frankie playing 'Old MacDonald Had a Farm'? That's the song we're singing!" Ada said.

Ella gathered her friends and came up with solutions for all their problems. Everything was running smoothly again.

Just then, Mrs. Briggs arrived. She didn't look well. She handed Ella a note saying that she had lost her voice and asking Ella to host the show. Ella had her doubts, but her friends encouraged her to do it. The show must go on!

Ella went onstage.

"Welcome to our super-spectacular talent show!" she said as the crowd clapped. Frankie played "Old MacDonald Had a Farm" on his one-man band, and Ada and Ida joined in by singing the song. They were the perfect accompaniment for Farmer Tiki and her Barnyard of Shadow Puppets!

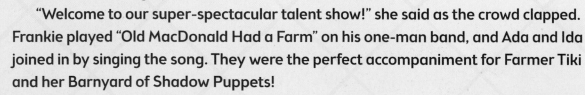

19

Finally, Belinda came onstage for her dance routine. One of the bananas fell off her hat, and she was about to trip over it!

Ella saw what was happening
from backstage. She had an idea.
"Magic hat, here we go!" she said,
and threw her hat into the air.

21

Ella's hat transformed into a giant elastic band. When Belinda slipped on the banana, the elastic band caught her. She was flung back out onto the stage and landed gracefully. The audience cheered. What an exciting performance!

Ella and her giant elastic
band had saved the day!

When the show was over, everyone cheered for the performers and Ella. Ella was the best host, introduction writer, and problem fixer— she had found her talents, after all!